HIDE-AND-SEEK
WITH
GRANDPA

Rob Lewis

First published in the United States of America in 1997
by **MONDO Publishing**
Originally published in the United Kingdom in 1997
by The Bodley Head Children's Books,
an imprint of Random House UK Ltd.

For information contact:
MONDO Publishing
One Plaza Road
Greenvale, New York 11548

Printed in Hong Kong
First Mondo Printing, November 1996
96 97 98 99 00 01   9 8 7 6 5 4 3 2 1

Library of Congress Cataloging-in-Publication Data
Lewis, Rob.
    Hide and seek with Grandpa / by Rob Lewis.
       p.   cm.
    Summary: In three stories, Finley, a young bear, keeps missing his very
active grandfather, plays hide-and-seek, and takes his grandfather a bag
of wiggly worms.
    ISBN 1-57255-226-3 (pbk : alk. paper)
    [1. Grandfathers—Fiction. 2. Bears—Fiction.] I. Title.
PZ7.L58785H1   1997
[Fic]—dc20   96-32108
                                                      CIP
                                                      AC

SPECIAL SUNDAYS

"Does Grandpa get lonely?" asked Finley.

"I don't think so," said Mom.

"But he lives all by himself," said Finley.

"I'm sure he keeps busy," said Mom.

Finley thought about Grandpa living
all by himself.

"I will visit him after school," he said.

"Ben is coming to play after school,"
said Mom.

"He can come another day," said Finley.

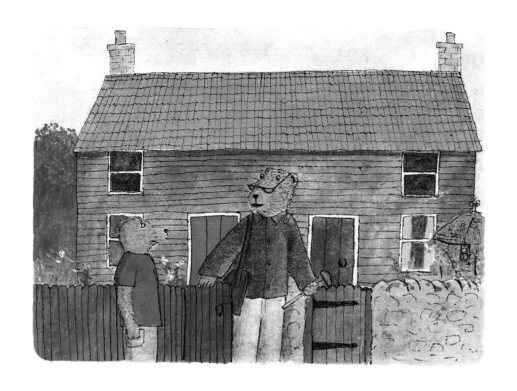

After school Finley went to Grandpa's
house. But Grandpa was just leaving.
"Sorry, Finley," said Grandpa. "I'm going
fossil hunting with Fred from next door."
"Oh," said Finley.

Finley went home. He telephoned Ben.

But Ben had gone out.

Finley sat all by himself.

"I will visit Grandpa tomorrow," he said.

"You are going skating with Sally and Joe tomorrow," Mom said.

"I can go with Ben on Friday," said Finley.

After school Finley went to Grandpa's house again. Grandpa was putting on his coat.

"Sorry, Finley," he said. "It's weight training night. I won't be back until late."
"Really," said Finley.

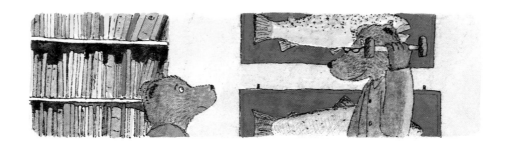

Finley went home. Sally and Joe had already gone skating. He sat all by himself. "I will try again tomorrow," he sighed. "You are going swimming with the Johnsons tomorrow," Mom said. "I can go swimming next week," said Finley.

After school Finley ran to Grandpa's house.
There were a lot of people outside.

"Sorry, Finley," said Grandpa. "We are all
going hang-gliding this evening."
"You're kidding!" said Finley.

Finley went home. He sat all by himself.

"Grandpa is very busy," said Mom.

"Grandpa is *too* busy!" said Finley crossly.

The next day Grandpa had tea with Fred.

"Finley came over three times this week," Grandpa said.

"Perhaps he is lonely," said Fred.

"I will visit him tonight," decided Grandpa.
"You have bricklaying class tonight,"
said Fred.
"I can miss one week," said Grandpa.

After school Grandpa went over to Finley's house.

"Sorry," said Mom. "Finley went skating with Ben."

Grandpa went home. He sat all by himself.

After skating, Finley telephoned Grandpa. "We are both very busy," said Finley. "We must choose a day when we are *not* busy." "We could meet on Sundays," said Grandpa. "OK," said Finley. "We will keep Sundays special."

HIDE-AND-SEEK

One Sunday, Grandpa and Finley were playing hide-and-seek.

"I will hide first," said Finley.

"OK," said Grandpa. "I will count to twenty."

"Count slowly," said Finley.

Grandpa counted to twenty, slowly.

Then he went to look for Finley.

Grandpa looked among the cabbages.

Then he looked in the garage.

Finley hid in the black currant bushes.

He waited a long time.

Grandpa was not very good at hide-and-seek. Finley went to look for him.

Grandpa was leaning over the fence. He was talking to Fred.

"Sorry, Finley," said Grandpa. "Fred was just showing me one of his fossils."

"I will hide again," said Finley.

"OK," said Grandpa.

Grandpa counted to twenty.

Finley hid in the greenhouse.

Grandpa looked in the garden shed and under the wheelbarrow.

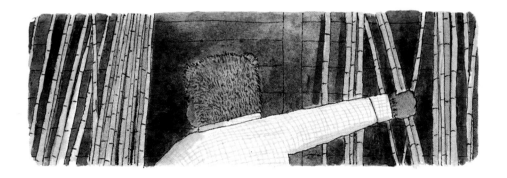

Then he wandered around to the front garden.

Finley waited in the greenhouse. He waited a long time.

Finally he went to look for Grandpa in the rhubarb.

Then he went around to the front garden. Grandpa was weeding.

"Um, sorry, Finley," said Grandpa. "I noticed a few weeds that needed to be pulled up."

"I will hide again," sighed Finley.

"I will count to twenty again," said Grandpa.

"Just count to ten," said Finley.

Grandpa counted to ten.

First Grandpa searched the compost heap.

Then he looked behind the deck chair.

Finley hid in the water barrel. He hid
for a long time. Then he heard a noise.
Someone was snoring. Grandpa had fallen
asleep in the deck chair.

"Wake up, Grandpa," shouted Finley.
"Sorry," said Grandpa, yawning. "I was
thinking about where you were hiding."
"I'm sure," said Finley. "Let's play
somewhere else."

"OK," said Grandpa. "I know a good place."
Grandpa led Finley to the bottom of the
garden. He opened the gate that led to
the woods.

"This is a better place," Grandpa said. "I will hide this time."

"Don't fall asleep," said Finley.

"Just start counting," said Grandpa.

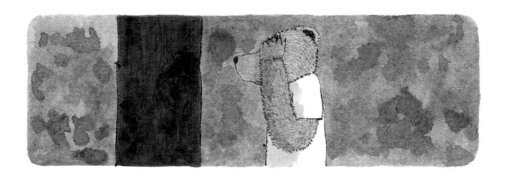

"Grandpa is not very good at hide-and-seek," said Finley to himself. "I will count to thirty this time."

Finley counted to thirty. Then he went to look for Grandpa.

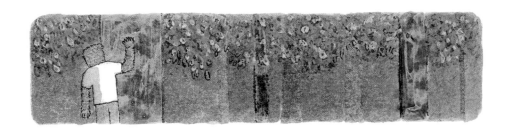

There were a lot of big trees to hide
behind. Grandpa was not behind any of
them. Finley went deeper into the woods.

He looked under bushes. He searched
piles of leaves. He peered under logs.
There was no sign of Grandpa.

"Grandpa got lost," Finley grumbled.

He followed the path back to the house.

But the path did not go back to the house.

"Now I'm lost," said Finley, worried.

"Found you!" said a voice. Finley looked up.
Grandpa was sitting in a tree. "I thought
you were doing the finding," Grandpa said.

WORMS

"Finley," called Mom. "Will you take
something over to Grandpa's house
for me?"

"OK, Mom," said Finley.

"It's on the table in the hall," called Mom.

"Fine," said Finley.

"Don't let them escape," said Mom.

"No, Mom," said Finley.

But Finley wasn't listening. He was busy
watching television.

When the program ended it was time
to go to Grandpa's house. Finley picked
up the plastic bag.

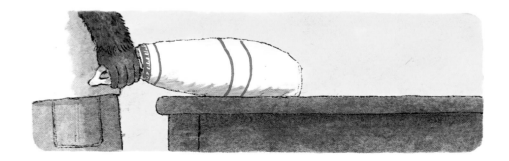

He walked to the bus stop. He waited in line.

A lady gave him a funny look. Something was tickling her leg.

"Stop tickling my leg," she said crossly.

"I'm not," said Finley.

Finley got on the bus.

A big lady sat down beside him. There was not much room for Finley. He looked out the window.

"Eeeeeek!" shrieked the lady. "There's a worm on my lap."

Finley looked in Grandpa's bag.

It was full of worms.

"Sorry," said Finley.

The worms kept escaping from the bag.

They were crawling all over the floor.

Soon everybody was shrieking. Finley

had to get off the bus.

He decided to walk to Grandpa's house.

On the way he bought a candy bar.

He sat down on a bench to eat it.

There was a baby in a stroller next to the bench.

"Hello," said Finley.

"Goo," said the baby.

Finley looked for a trash basket for his
candy wrapper.

The baby looked at Grandpa's plastic bag.

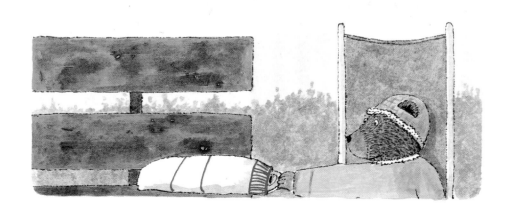

Finley put the wrapper in the basket.

The baby put a hand in Grandpa's bag.

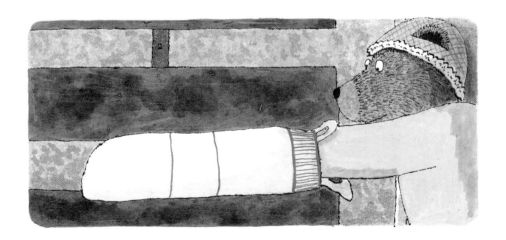

Finley ate the last of his candy bar.

The baby ate a worm.

"Oh no!" cried Finley.

"Goo!" said the baby. Finley felt sick.

Finley hurried to Grandpa's house.
Birds flew around his head. They wanted
the worms in Grandpa's bag.

"Go away birds!" shouted Finley.

At last Finley got to Grandpa's house.

"Here are your worms," said Finley.

"I will catch some big fish with these,"
said Grandpa. "Thank you."

"No problem," said Finley.

"Could you bring something next week,
too?" asked Grandpa.

"Not more worms," said Finley, worried.

"Not worms," said Grandpa. "Maggots."

"Oh no!" groaned Finley.